The Elves
and the Shoemaker

Retold by Eric Suben
Illustrated by Jerry Smath

A GOLDEN BOOK • NEW YORK
Western Publishing Company, Inc., Racine, Wisconsin 53404

Once upon a time there was a kind shoemaker. Though he worked very hard, he grew poorer and poorer. At last he had only enough leather left to make one more pair of shoes.

One winter night he cut the leather out for shoes, but he was too tired to go any further. He left the leather on his workbench and decided to stitch the shoes together the next morning.

The shoemaker went to bed not knowing what he and his wife would do once the leather was used up. They had no money to buy more. Despite their troubles, the shoemaker and his wife slept soundly that night.

Early the next morning the shoemaker woke up
and got dressed. Then he went into the shop to
make the last pair of shoes.

Once he sat down at his workbench, the
shoemaker thought he must be dreaming. He
blinked his eyes. He blinked them again. But it was
not a dream. On the very spot where he had left
the leather the night before, there was a pair of
beautiful, well-made shoes—all finished!

He called his wife into the shop and showed her the shoes. "They're splendid!" she exclaimed. "But when did you make them?"

"I didn't make them," the shoemaker replied. "I found them here this morning."

The shoemaker put the shoes in the window, hoping that someone would buy them. Soon the door swung open, and a fine gentleman walked into the shop.

"I must have these wonderful shoes," he said. "I've never seen any like them. The stitches are so small and delicate!"

The shoemaker sold the shoes to the gentleman, who paid a very high price for them.

With the money, the shoemaker was able to buy enough leather to make two more pairs of shoes. And he had enough left over to buy a soup bone for dinner.

That night the shoemaker cut out the leather. But he was very hungry, and he could smell the soup his wife was cooking. "I'll make the shoes tomorrow," he said, and he went to eat dinner.

The next morning he found two pairs of elegant
shoes on his workbench. He showed them to his wife.
    "Who can be making these marvelous shoes?"
she said.
    The shoemaker shook his head in wonder.

Once again the shoemaker placed the shoes in
the window. He didn't have long to wait before the
door to the shop swung open. This time there were
two customers, and they both paid handsomely for
the fine shoes.

Now the shoemaker had enough money to buy leather for four more pairs of shoes.

Things went on this way for some time. Every night the shoemaker cut the leather and went to sleep. And every morning he found more beautiful shoes on his workbench.

The shoemaker and his wife were no longer poor. They sold so many pairs of shoes that little by little they began to save some money.

One evening the shoemaker said to his wife, "It's nearly Christmas, and we still don't know who is sewing all these shoes for us. We cannot go another day without finding out who it is."

So together the shoemaker and his wife thought of a plan. Instead of going to sleep that night, they hid behind a curtain in the shop.

At midnight two tiny elves skipped through the door into the room. The shoemaker and his wife watched in amazement as the elves quickly began to stitch and sew.

Soon the bench was filled with handsome new
shoes. But the moment their work was finished,
the elves vanished.

The shoemaker and his wife were astonished. They decided they must do something for the tiny creatures who had been so kind to them.

"The elves were not wearing any coats or hats or shoes," said the wife. "The poor little things must get very cold at this time of year."

So the shoemaker and his wife made two tiny suits of clothing for the elves.

The next night they laid the little clothes they had made on the table. Then they hid behind the curtain once again.

Just at midnight the elves came into the shop.
When they saw the clothes, they were overjoyed.
They hurried to try on their outfits and found that
everything fit them perfectly.

In their brand-new clothes, the elves danced
around the room and sang a merry song.

At last the elves danced out the door of the shoemaker's shop, never to return again.

The thoughtful shoemaker and his good wife had repaid kindness with kindness. They never wanted for anything and lived happily for the rest of their days.